Farah Rocks

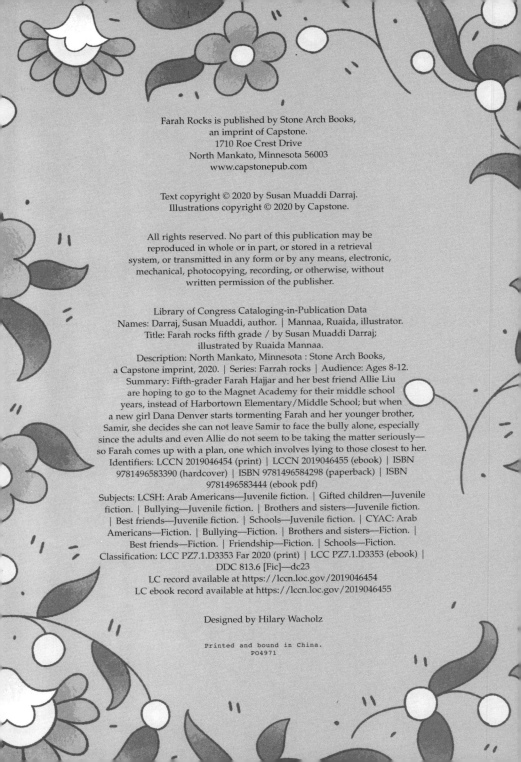

Farah Rocks is published by Stone Arch Books,
an imprint of Capstone.
1710 Roe Crest Drive
North Mankato, Minnesota 56003
www.capstonepub.com

Library of Congress Cataloging-in-Publication Data
Names: Darraj, Susan Muaddi, author. | Mannaa, Ruaida, illustrator.
Title: Farah rocks fifth grade / by Susan Muaddi Darraj;
illustrated by Ruaida Mannaa.
Description: North Mankato, Minnesota : Stone Arch Books,
a Capstone imprint, 2020. | Series: Farrah rocks | Audience: Ages 8-12.
Summary: Fifth-grader Farah Hajjar and her best friend Allie Liu
are hoping to go to the Magnet Academy for their middle school
years, instead of Harbortown Elementary/Middle School; but when
a new girl Dana Denver starts tormenting Farah and her younger brother,
Samir, she decides she can not leave Samir to face the bully alone, especially
since the adults and even Allie do not seem to be taking the matter seriously—
so Farah comes up with a plan, one which involves lying to those closest to her.
Identifiers: LCCN 2019046454 (print) | LCCN 2019046455 (ebook) | ISBN
9781496583390 (hardcover) | ISBN 9781496584298 (paperback) | ISBN
9781496583444 (ebook pdf)
Subjects: LCSH: Arab Americans—Juvenile fiction. | Gifted children—Juvenile
fiction. | Bullying—Juvenile fiction. | Brothers and sisters—Juvenile fiction.
| Best friends—Juvenile fiction. | Schools—Juvenile fiction. | CYAC: Arab
Americans—Fiction. | Bullying—Fiction. | Brothers and sisters—Fiction. |
Best friends—Fiction. | Friendship—Fiction. | Schools—Fiction.
Classification: LCC PZ7.1.D3353 Far 2020 (print) | LCC PZ7.1.D3353 (ebook) |
DDC 813.6 [Fic]—dc23
LC record available at https://lccn.loc.gov/2019046454
LC ebook record available at https://lccn.loc.gov/2019046455

Designed by Hilary Wacholz

Printed and bound in China.
PO4971

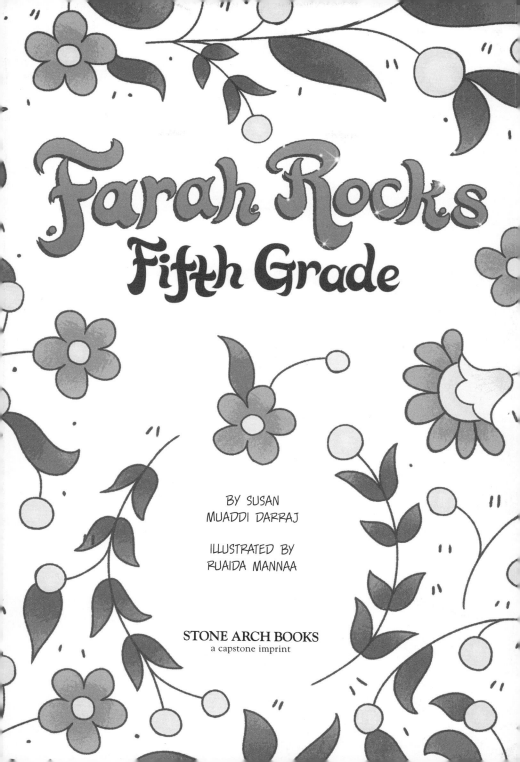

Farah Rocks
Fifth Grade

BY SUSAN
MUADDI DARRAJ

ILLUSTRATED BY
RUAIDA MANNAA

STONE ARCH BOOKS
a capstone imprint

CHAPTER 1

"Faw-wah, where's Mama?" asks my little brother, Samir. He is holding his green light-up sneakers with Tommy Turtle on the sides. Mama bought them at a yard sale because they looked new. But right now, they look awful. The bottoms are caked with mud.

"You should have worn your boots outside," I tell him. It's the last day of winter break. The snow has turned all mushy and brown.

"Biddee Mama!" he says.

"On the phone," I explain. I don't say it will probably be a long time before she's done. That's because she's talking to Mrs. Liu, the mother of my Official Best

Friend, Allie. And they're talking about their favorite subject—the Magnet Academy.

For two years, our moms have been talking about Magnet. But lately, because our applications are due in six weeks, it's been even worse than usual. Allie and I are fifth graders at Harbortown Public School. For middle school, we're hoping to get into Magnet. It's a public school, but with a special focus on science and math. Allie and I have heard that Magnet students end up getting jobs as astronauts and chemists and heart surgeons.

Samir groans, snapping me out of my thoughts about Magnet. "I want clean sneakews for school tomowwow!"

"Come on," I tell him. We head to the kitchen. If Mama is still on the phone, I can clean the sneakers for him. I help my parents a lot in taking care of Samir.

Baba is flipping pancakes at the stove. He likes to make breakfast food for dinner, or dinner food for breakfast. Sometimes he even grills hamburgers at nine in the morning. He says the chef makes the rules.

Mama is leaning against the counter, her cell phone to her ear. "What science classes should they take?" she says. Pause. "Yes, I agree. And we'll sign them both up for Latin, of course."

Allie and I are really excited for Latin. One of the reasons Allie and I are Official Best Friends is because, in second grade, Harbortown labeled us "gifted" and put us in Advanced Academic (AA) classes. The school says "gifted" means that we are really smart. But for us, "gifted" means we just get more homework than everyone else.

Even though I don't like the word *gifted*, I *am* thrilled about going to Magnet. I've already thought of a dozen ideas for my essay. But I refuse to work on it tonight, I decide. This is the last day of my winter break. I want to enjoy it.

Of course, I think, as I start looking under the sink

for a scrub brush, *cleaning Samir's muddy sneakers isn't exactly* fun.

Baba flips a pancake and tells Mama, "Food's almost ready."

Mama nods at Baba. "Maybe we'll get our families together for dinner soon," she says into the phone. Pause. "Thanks. Good night, Lin."

After Mama hangs up, she sings to herself in Arabic, looking all dreamy. She snaps out of it when she asks me what I'm doing under the sink. I point to Samir.

"Your shoes, Samir!" she exclaims, horrified. "How can you wear these to al-madrasa tomorrow?"

"Sowwy!" He has trouble pronouncing his r's. It's not a huge problem, compared to all the health problems he's had.

"Thanks, Farah, but I'll clean them myself later. Go put them by the back door," Mama says. "Ready to eat?"

"Yes!" we say together. Eating Baba's pancakes is even more awesome than hearing him say "bancakes." In Arabic, the letters *p* and *v* don't exist. Baba just replaces them both with the letter *b*. It's the closest he can get when he's speaking English. Mama came to the United States when she was my age, but Baba came when he was twenty-eight.

"Farah has to comblete her abblication for Magnet," Baba says. He puts a plate heaped with fluffy pancakes on the table. "Did you start?" he asks me, pouring everyone a glass of juice.

"I just have to write the essay," I say. I use my knife to saw through a stack of three pancakes, oozing with syrup.

"What are you witing about?" Samir asks.

"Why Magnet should accept me. I'm not sure what to say: Because I'm smart? Or because I'm awesome? Or because I'm amazing . . ."

"Or maybe because you are so confident," Baba says with a grin.

Samir pats my shoulder. "Those are good ideas," he says seriously.

In Samir's world, I'm like a hero. Most kids think

little brothers are annoying. Not me. I'm glad that he thinks I'm his cool big sister.

Samir is six years younger than I am. My parents were excited for another baby, but Samir arrived too quickly: three whole months early. Even though I was only in preschool, I knew this was bad news.

He stayed in the hospital for three months. The doctors thought he might not live. Mama and Baba made a promise then. If Samir would just be okay, they would donate a new stained-glass window to our church. That's St. Jude's, the Orthodox church that all the Arabs like us attend.

And Samir did come home, looking like a tiny, bald bird. So my parents bought the window, which is taller than my dad—and really expensive. In fact, we're still paying for it. It's one reason why my parents worry about money. Another reason is all Samir's therapy, which costs tons of money. He needs extra help, and luckily Harbortown is great. He gets pulled out of kindergarten class to work on his speech. And once a week, an occupational therapist helps him. They work on holding a pencil and printing his letters.

"Well, Farah?" Baba says to me now. "When will you finish it?"

"Baba," I whine, "it's the last day of winter break. I'll start it this week, I promise!"

"Inshallah, you will—" Mama says.

"I know, I know," I interrupt her. "Inshallah I will get accepted."

"We will bray," Baba says, then stuffs a forkful of pancakes into his mouth.

CHAPTER 2

Before Baba leaves for work at the quarry the next morning, he wishes Samir and me good luck on our first day of the quarter.

"Wish me luck too," he says. "I'm hoping to get a raise this year. I will find out maybe this week."

"Good luck!" we both sing out.

"Baba, can you check on the labyrinth on your way home?" I ask. Over the summer, the Harbortown Library hired an artist to build a labyrinth. It's a large walking maze shaped in a circle in the library's back field. I've been waiting for months for them to complete it. I really want to know if it's close to being done.

"Okay. Take care of your brother, Farah." Baba winks and heads out the door.

Samir and I are eating hummus for breakfast when Mama puts the Magnet Academy application on the kitchen table next to me. "When you get home after al-madrasa," she says, "you need to work on this."

I roll my eyes, making sure she doesn't see me. It's annoying whenever someone reminds me of something I already *know* I have to do.

Fifteen minutes later, Samir and I are sitting on the bus. Suddenly everyone starts talking excitedly. It's because at the second stop, there's a new girl. At first I think that she must be getting on the wrong bus. She wears bright-pink lip gloss. She is taller than our bus driver, Ms. Juniper, and has long, red hair in thick curls.

If she does belong on our bus, I feel sorry for her. There are many reasons Bus Sixty-Two stinks.

1. Jake Montana, who picks his nose, rides the Sixty-Two.

2. So do the Beckinson twins, who fight the whole ride and pull each other's hair.

3. Bridget Greko also rides the Sixty-Two. (But I don't really want to talk about her. We stopped being friends a long time ago.)

4. I better not forget Winston Suarez, who tattles on everybody. Including me when I used to sneak up to sit with Samir. My little brother was just starting kindergarten and was new to the bus. But older kids have to sit in the back. Winston squealed to Ms. Juniper, who is shaped like a giant bowling pin.

5. Another thing: We have the worst bus driver in Harbortown.

"Older kids sit in the back!" Ms. Juniper bellowed at me that day from her tiny bowling-pin head.

"But he's my little brother!" I protested.

"Move on back!" she shouted.

So if you're going to be a new kid, Bus Sixty-Two is probably the worst welcome.

Jake pulls his finger out of his nose and uses it to point to the new girl as she climbs aboard. "Who's that?" he asks me.

"Don't know," I say.

"I thought you knew everything, Farah Rocks," he says.

I've been called Farah Rocks since kindergarten. Our last name, *Hajjar*, means "rocks" in Arabic. We got that name because my baba's family were stonecutters in Jerusalem.

The new girl looks like she doesn't want to be here. I want to tell her it will soon get worse, because this is Bus Sixty-Two. But she'll figure it out when the Beckinson twins start fighting.

Samir sits two rows ahead of me, swinging his legs. "Kapow!" he says under his breath. That's what Tommy Turtle says on his show. "Kapow! Kapow!"

When the new girl walks by, she stumbles over his

feet. "Hey!" she snaps. Her voice is whisper-weird, like she has a sore throat. "Watch it!"

"Sorry," I say, quickly standing up.

But before I get there, Samir reaches out and tugs on one of her long, shiny, red curls. "Pwetty!" he says.

"Are you making fun of me?" she growls. And then she does something you're not allowed to do on the bus—or anywhere. She smacks his hand away from her hair. Hard.

Samir yelps and pulls his hand back. Everyone else goes quiet, staring at us. I notice Ms. Juniper glance back in her long mirror, maybe surprised that it's suddenly as silent as a cemetery.

"What are you—an idiot?" the new girl asks Samir.

"Hey!" I say. I feel like I've been punched.

Samir curls up in his seat like a shrimp and tucks his hand under his chin. He always does that when he's upset.

I step into the bus aisle to defend my little brother. I have to look up at the new girl because when I look straight ahead, I am staring at the buttons of her red coat. "He thinks your hair is pretty!" I explain.

"Sit down," she says fiercely. Her mouth looks like a pink slash across her face.

I stay on my feet.

"Sit down," she whispers again. What a terrible, scary whisper.

Holy hummus, I think. And then I sit down.

She keeps walking toward the rear while people around us snicker. The Beckinson twins say together, "Duuuuude." The kindergarten kids look back at me, wide-eyed. Winston stays quiet for once. Doesn't he think *this* would be a good time to tattle?

The new girl sits in the back next to Bridget, who phony-gushes, "I *love* your hair!"

I move up to sit with Samir and hold his hand for the rest of the ride. He seems terrified. When we get to school, I rush us both off the bus before everyone else.

"Wait your turn!" hollers Ms. Juniper, but I ignore her today.

CHAPTER 3

At lunch, Allie shares what she's learned about the new girl. "Name: Dana Denver," she begins, as we unpack our lunches. "She's in my health class. Mr. Montgomery had her introduce herself." Health and PE are the only classes that are not AA and that Allie and I don't have together. For those classes, we switch teachers.

Allie pulls her red plastic chopsticks out of her lunch pouch. "Dana just moved here from *Texas.*"

My brain rattles off some facts. Texas, the Lone Star State. Looks like it has a chimney. Second-largest

U.S. state in terms of area. Capital: Austin. A few years ago, Baba bought me a U.S. map place mat. I studied it every morning while eating my hummus. Eventually I memorized all fifty states.

"She's so tall," Allie says. "When Mr. Montgomery asked her to stand up and tell everyone about herself, I thought she was already standing up!"

I burst into giggles.

"So what happened on the bus?" Allie asks.

I tell Allie the whole story. When I'm done, her mouth drops open. "Wait, you *sat down*?" she asks, horrified.

I am also suddenly horrified.

"Well, what was I supposed to do?" I grumble. "Fight her? She's taller than most adults I know."

Allie thinks about it. "No," she says finally. "Fighting gets you suspended from the bus." Then she asks, "Didn't Bridget do anything?"

"No," I grumble. "You know how Bridget is."

"You always think she's so terrible," Allie says,

rolling her eyes. "She's in my health class too. She's pretty nice to me."

Bridget used to be our friend, until she changed in third grade. I guess I was hurt by it more than Allie. I change the subject, because I don't like talking about Bridget. "What else did Dana say?" I ask.

Allie ticks her fingers on her left hand. "Plays basketball. Broke a record for swimming at her old school. Favorite color is denim—"

"Denim is not a color!" I interrupt.

"Fact. Also, she rides horses. She just got her own pony for Christmas, but they left him in Texas." Allie pauses, her chopsticks poised in the air. "I think maybe that part is made up. Who buys a horse and then leaves him in Texas?"

We both think about it for a bit, then agree that Dana *must* be lying about owning a horse.

"Well, Dana and her imaginary horse won't be at Magnet. I'm so excited for next year," says Allie.

"Yeah," I say happily. "And we won't have to deal

with *that* anymore." I point to the Beckinson twins, who are having a sword fight with their corn dogs.

"Bonus!" she agrees. Together, we watch Winston, who raises his hand to tattle on them. The lunch monitor, who walks around handing out napkins and sporks, waves Winston away. She's heard him tattle a million times.

However, my smile falls right off my face when I turn my head and see Dana. She's standing by the window and staring outside. My heart starts pounding. I know what she's looking at. Right now, Samir's kindergarten class is on the playground.

Dana points outside while speaking to Bridget and some other girls at their table. Whatever she says makes them all crack up.

I have to know what she's saying. I stand up and pretend as if I'm going to throw my napkin in the trash can, which is next to Dana's table.

Even though her back is to me, I hear her now. "Why do they have *those* kids at this school?"

I imagine what she is seeing. Maybe Samir is sitting on the mulch, his hand tucked under his chin. Maybe his friend Ana is having a hard time climbing the steps to the slide because of her leg braces. Maybe Thomas is sitting in his wheelchair, drawing a picture.

Dana shudders, as if something is grossing her out. The other kids gather at the window to watch and roll their eyes. Bridget is there too. As I learned a long time ago, she never misses a chance to be popular, even if it equals being mean.

Suddenly Dana turns her head and sees me. I hurry back to my table. There is a tight ball of fear in my chest.

"What's wrong, Farah?" Allie asks.

"The new girl—I think she's making fun of some of Samir's friends," I say.

Allie shakes her head. "I doubt it."

"I don't think so," I say. I'm laser-sharp about how

other kids look at Samir's friends. When she said "those kids," I know what she meant.

"Well, then you should tell someone," she says logically.

Right.

I walk up to the lunch monitor. "Excuse me?"

"You need a spork?" she asks me tiredly.

"No. Um, that girl right there—" I say, turning to make sure Dana doesn't see me pointing. "She's making fun of the kids on the playground."

"Sweetie, that's not a huge deal. Please sit down, okay? The bell's about to ring." And she walks away, just like that.

I stand there, stunned. The lady looked at me as if I was Winston, complaining about small stuff.

I report back to Allie, who shrugs. "Forget it," she says. "Nobody got hurt. Let's go."

"But, Allie, she's making fun of my brother."

"Well, we can tell Dana's teacher."

I think about what to do as I pack up my lunch.

I could talk to her teacher, but what would happen? He'll just talk to Dana. She will say she didn't do it. I'll say she did.

Maybe they'll call in her mom for a conference. She'll say Dana is an angel. I'll say she's not. Nobody will be able to prove anything. They might even tell me what the lunch monitor just did, that it's not a big deal. And that means nothing will be solved. Even worse: Dana will hate me for complaining about her.

"Come on, Farah," Allie says. "We're going to be late for class."

Doesn't she understand that this situation is bothering me? I think. *I'm upset right now, but she is already packed up and ready to head to class.*

"I'm coming," I say, trying to hide my annoyance.

CHAPTER 4

Thankfully, Dana is not on the bus home. *Her* new Official Best Friend, Bridget, tells everyone that Dana has basketball practice. "She'll only be on the bus in the morning," she says.

Usually I read my book of Greek mythology on the ride home, but today I'm too freaked out to read. It was really weird to have the lunch monitor wave me off as if I was complaining about something that wasn't a big deal. Maybe when teachers and parents talk about bullying, they're talking about hitting or shoving or saying mean things to people on social media.

Bus Sixty-Two stops in front of our small townhouse

at 5 Hollow Woods Lane. Baba wanted this house, according to my mother, because *hollow* sounds like *hilou*, which means "pretty" in Arabic. He said it was a good omen.

My dad is really into names. *Farah* means "joy," because when I was born, they were pretty thrilled. (I can't blame them.) *Samir*, in Arabic, means "someone who's a lot of fun to be with." And yes, that's my little brother one hundred percent.

That's why it hurt to see people at lunch making fun of him and his friends.

I help Samir hop off the last step on the bus. Mama's at work, so I unlock the door with my key. Since Mama started as a cashier at Harbortown Supermart, she usually gets home about an hour after we do.

We follow our after-school routine: Put our shoes in the basket by the door, because Mama doesn't let us wear them inside, then have a snack and relax before homework.

In the kitchen, I give Samir some crayons and paper

while I wash and chop apples. Mama's new schedule means that I take care of him more and more. I don't mind, because my parents worry about money. They think I don't know this, but come on. Baba sighs whenever he checks the mail and sees more bills. You don't have to be gifted to put it all together.

While I chop, I listen to Samir hum while drawing a picture of what might be a yellow bus. He's working on his grip, carefully sketching black circles as tires.

"Emmms?" he asks me hopefully when I put the apple slices in a bowl before him. "Please?"

"Not too many," I say in my secret-soft voice. From the bottom cabinet, I pull out a bag of M&Ms—his favorite.

Like I said, I'm his hero.

He excitedly separates them into piles by color: red, green, yellow, blue, one stray orange candy. Then he counts how many he has in each pile.

He's getting really good with his numbers. I'll tell Mama later. She keeps a notebook where she writes down information like this to share with his doctors.

While he eats, I notice a note on the far counter.

Dear Farah,
Please start working on the essay for the Magnet
Academy. Also, please set the oven to 375 degrees.
When it's preheated, put the chicken in.
Love,
Mama

P.S.: Don't let Samir eat any candy! It will ruin his
appetite.

Holy hummus, I think. *Guess I won't tell her about the M&Ms after all.*

Mama left the essay directions under her note. I read them over for the hundredth time. *In three hundred words or less,* it says, *explain what you can contribute to Magnet Academy's student body.*

Part of me wants to say that I can't imagine *not* going to Magnet. Mama has been dreaming about it. Allie has been dreaming about it. And to tell the truth, so have I.

I've heard all about the laboratories. And they give every student a laptop. There's a science fair every month. Allie and I have already agreed that we'll be partners for all of them.

While Samir colors and eats illegal M&Ms, I take out my newest rock and polish it with a soft cloth. Polishing my rock collection helps me relax and think. Harbortown is really boring for me. Can I say that in my essay? I mean, it's true.

Here's an example. Today in science, we looked at leaves under a microscope. I found a dead fly on the windowsill and put it under the glass, but Winston (who else?) told on me. Mr. Richie is my favorite teacher of all time, but even he told me to throw the fly away and focus on the leaf.

Allie and I have been using her father's microscope

to look at leaves since second grade. I've studied tons of leaves. Guess what I've *never* seen up close before?

A dead bug.

I'd like to be in a school where they get as excited about that as I do. How can I explain that in an essay? Also, I'm pretty sure there won't be girls like Dana and Bridget at a school like Magnet. That's another thing I don't know how to explain.

When Mama comes home, I'm about to tell her what happened on the bus. But right away, she asks about my essay. *Again.*

"Well, I've been thinking about it," I explain before she can complain. "Polishing helps me do that."

"So you're just writing in your head?"

"Exactly!"

"Well, that's good. Then you should be able to wash the breakfast dishes. That's polishing too."

I groan, but Samir laughs—until Mama tells him that he's now old enough to dry.

CHAPTER 5

For the next few mornings on the bus, Dana pokes Samir every time she passes by him. Usually she does it so quickly that he doesn't even know who it was. She laughs, along with Bridget, at his confusion.

Allie says to tell the bus driver what's going on. But how can I talk to Ms. Juniper? She's not exactly friendly. Other bus drivers give out lollipops on Fridays. Ms. Juniper hands out stickers from a roll that's so old the stickers don't even stick anymore. And she's always yelling at us to hurry up as we get on and off the bus.

I decide that no matter what Ms. Juniper's rules are, I need to sit next to my brother. Every day I wait until she closes the big door and drives off from our bus stop. Then I sneak up and sit beside him.

That Friday, I am again sitting with Samir on the bus. I keep my head down so Ms. Juniper won't notice. "Look outside," I tell him. The mist clings to the trees, and everything looks ghostly white. "There's so much fog today. It's like a big cloud fell from the sky!"

At the next stop, I see Dana. She's carrying her red backpack and wearing tall, black cowboy boots. I imagine those boots stomping on my head.

Gripping Samir's hand, I pretend to read my mythology book. Tremors ripple through the bus as Dana climbs the steps and heads down the aisle.

"Dana! Back here!" Bridget shouts.

However, when Dana reaches my seat, she stops. I keep looking at my book—the story of Athena turning Arachne into a spider.

"Take your seats!" Ms. Juniper calls from the front.

But Dana still hovers over us. "Hey!" she says, poking me on the shoulder.

Slowly, I look up at her freckled face, wishing I could turn her into a spider.

"Are you his sister?"

I nod, because my voice doesn't seem to work.

"What's your name?" she asks in her terrible whisper.

"Farah," I reply in my own whisper.

"Fa-roh? Like . . . like *pharaoh*?" She snickers. "Like someone from Egypt?"

I almost tell her that my parents were born in a place close to Egypt. But she doesn't really care.

"Seats!" Ms. Juniper bellows again.

Dana bends down. Her face is so close that I can count her freckles and see the creases in her pink lip gloss. "I see you staring at me during lunch. Stay out of my way, Pharaoh." And then she is gone.

For the rest of the ride, that name, *Pharaoh*, bugs me. It's the first time anyone at Harbortown has made fun of me because I have an Arabic name. Why didn't I answer her, and tell her to not call me that?

Because you're scared, I answer myself.

By the time we arrive at school, I'm stuck in a daydream in which Dana stuffs me into my locker.

"Let's go, you two," says Ms. Juniper, looking at Samir and me in her long mirror. "You're the last ones off."

"Sorry," I say. *Maybe I should tell Ms. Juniper,* I think. *I mean, she probably doesn't know. She can't worry about what kids are doing on the bus when she's driving the bus.* As we walk toward the front of the bus, I decide to speak up. "Ms. Juniper, the tall, redheaded girl who sits in the back is bullying us."

"Oh, I don't believe that." She turns in her seat to face me. "She seems like a nice girl. What's she doing?"

"She's calling us names."

"Like?"

"Like . . . like . . . *pharaoh.*"

She scrunches her eyebrows together. "I don't get it. Is she touching you or hitting you?"

"Umm . . . no."

"She slapped my hand one time," Samir pipes up.

"Yes! That's true!" I add, glad my brother has a good memory.

"Well, she told me about that, and said *you* pulled *her* hair." Ms. Juniper wags a finger at Samir. "On her first day too. It's hard to be the new kid. You should be nicer to her."

I can't think of anything to say. I'm shocked. Dana is more clever—and sneaky—than I thought. No matter what I say now, Ms. Juniper won't believe me.

"I can't hold up the other buses," Ms. Juniper says. She pulls on her lever to open the door.

"Okay." I sigh and head down the steps after Samir.

"And by the way," she adds, before closing the door, "no sitting with the kindergarten kids! I won't tell you again. And try not to make a big deal about such a little thing. Bullying is serious, you know."

"Fawah, is that giwl a bully?" Samir asks me as we hurry to the school's front door.

"No. Don't worry about her," I say. "I'll take care of it."

. . .

Later that afternoon, during science, Allie, four other AA kids, and I are called to the guidance counselor's office.

There are fifteen students in AA. The six of us are the only ones with grades high enough to apply to Magnet. Winston is one of them. He's almost as good in his classes as he is at tattling. Lauren is another student who's been chosen to apply. She has been playing the violin since she was five, and she's awesome at it. Adaego is with us too. She's a math whiz. Her parents hired a special teacher to challenge her. She's doing trigonometry now.

Enrique is the last of our crew. He is a jock who plays basketball, football, soccer, and baseball. He's also supersmart and nice. His father pushes him hard, hoping one day Enrique will get a college scholarship. All that does is stress out Enrique. Today, he's wearing a Hurricanes jersey. "I bet you got that for Christmas," I say as we walk down the hall.

"How'd you know?"

"There's a clue," I say. I point to the round sticker on his shoulder that says *large*.

"Ha! You *are* a genius, Farah Rocks," he says, peeling it off.

"Hold on," I tell everyone, stopping at the water fountain.

"You can't do that!" Winston says as I take a drink.

Enrique and Allie also take sips.

"We're supposed to go right to the office," Winston complains. He worries about everything.

"Calm down," says Adaego.

"But Mr. Richie said to go *straight* there," Winston insists.

"Holy hummus," I tell him. "Chill out."

"I'm allergic to hummus," he says. "Come on. She's waiting."

I know the guidance counselor, Ms. Loft, pretty well. She helps Mama with all of Samir's paperwork. In her office, she's sitting behind her big desk. Back in October, she had a baby girl. There are pictures of her all over the desk and the windowsill.

"Welcome, everybody," she says. "Take a seat." There's a dark food stain on the shoulder of her red jacket. A pencil is jammed in her bun to keep it from falling apart.

"As you know, we selected the six of you to apply to Magnet. We feel you each have a strong chance to be accepted," Ms. Loft says. "Our school has a solid record. In the last five years," she adds as proof, "thirty-two out of thirty-eight Harbortown students who applied were accepted."

Lauren says, "This is really exciting!"

"I hope we *all* get in," says Enrique. Everyone else lets out a small cheer.

"That's our goal," says Ms. Loft. "I hope you're working on your essays. And remember—Magnet wants all your grades, including for this quarter, which ends in a few weeks."

Ms. Loft looks around carefully at each of us. Then she asks, in a serious voice, "Are you all up to the challenge of the Magnet Academy?"

Everyone shouts, "Yes!"

I nod, even though I feel a flash of worry. For the past two years, Magnet is everything I've wanted. It's been my main focus.

But that was before Dana Denver.

I can't help but wonder: *What will happen to Samir if I leave him alone here next year?*

After the meeting, I ask Ms. Loft if I can stay for a few extra minutes.

She smiles at me after everyone leaves and asks, "What's up, Farah?"

"It's about the new girl at Harbortown, Dana Denver," I start to say.

She interrupts me. "Oh, I'm so glad you met her! Did you know she's my new neighbor?"

"N–neighbor?"

"Yes! Sweet girl. Her mom is also very nice. Dana plays basketball with my daughter sometimes." She shrugs. "She's lovely. Have you gotten to know her?"

"Um, yeah. Yeah, I have," I reply, then say that I need to get back to class.

"But what did you want to ask me?" She seems confused as she hands me a new hall pass.

"Never mind. You answered it," I tell her. As I walk back to class, I think that Dana may just have every adult I know completely fooled.

CHAPTER 6

During "shursh" (that's how Baba says *church*), the only place where Samir will usually be quiet is on Baba's lap. Mama sits next to me, listening to Father Alex.

We all stand when he reads from the Gospel. Baba lifts Samir, who rests his head on Baba's shoulder and dozes off. Samir's feet, stuffed in his Tommy Turtle sneakers, dangle in the air.

Behind Father Alex is the stained-glass window my parents bought. I really hate that window. As the Gospel is being read, I count up how many family vacations and light-up sneakers and summer art camps that window has cost me. That window means I wear every

Halloween costume two years in a row (the first year it's too big, and the second year it's too tight). That window is why we never, ever eat at a restaurant unless it's a kids-eat-free deal.

When we sit again, Samir murmurs something in his sleep. Baba raises his eyebrows at me.

I nod yes. I know what he's asking. A second later, he shifts Samir onto my lap.

"Shou aziza bintkoum," one of the aunties whispers behind me in Arabic. Baba grins at her. He thanks her for saying what a nice girl I am.

During the rest of the mass, I hold Samir. I feel angry about how those kids at school laughed at him. I wish I could protect him like this, all the time, from everything.

. . .

Later that evening, Mama cooks our big meal of the week: koosa mahshi. It's yellow squash stuffed with rice and beef, served over hot rice and roasted almonds. Sunday is the only day we have a real family dinner because of Mama's new job and all Baba's extra hours.

While we eat, Mama makes us all share one good thing that happened this week. "It's a Hajjar tradition," she insists.

Baba starts. "Well," he begins, rubbing the palms of his hands together, "I had a rough week, actually. No raise this year. Again."

I feel terrible. I know my parents hoped he'd get more money this year.

"*But* I do have some good news. Two things, actually." He holds up two fingers. "Is that okay?"

"Of cawse!" says Samir generously. We all laugh.

"I think Farah will like number one," Baba says. "They finished building the labyrinth at the library."

Finally! "Let's go as soon as it opens!" I say.

"What's the second thing?" Mama asks.

"We found some red stone yesterday," Baba says.

"Look." He pulls his phone out of his pocket and opens the photo. "See how bretty?" He hands the phone to me.

He's right—it's a beautiful lava-red.

Mama nods at me. "Something good," she prompts.

"Allie and I found the beginning of a bird's nest in the maple tree at recess," I say.

We found it one day when I convinced Allie to stay away from the monkey bars. That's where Dana and Bridget hang out. Allie wanted to talk to Bridget, who's being nicer than ever in health class, but I guess she joined me since I *am* her Official Best Friend. As we stood by the tree, we looked up and saw a clump of twigs and grass blades swirled up between the branches.

I haven't told my parents about Dana. Not yet. I don't like to add more stress. So all I say is, "We're going to keep track as the bird builds it."

"That's very special," Mama says. She touches Samir's shoulder gently. "Your turn."

"Thewe's a new giwl on the bus," he says.

I freeze, wondering what he will say.

"Mean?" Baba asks, smiling.

I almost think Baba is saying Dana is mean, but he's saying the word for *who* in Arabic. But the word sure does fit.

"She has wed haiwh," Samir adds.

"Ahmar," Mama says. "How unique."

"She's a big giwl, like Fah-wah."

They both turn to me. "Is she a fifth grader?" Baba asks.

"Not sure." I don't want Samir to mention what Dana is doing on the bus, so I change the subject by telling Mama, "Your turn."

"Well," Mama says, "my job can give me more hours." She smiles at Baba. "That will help a bit. But I will need Farah to help even more with Samir, because I will be working late most days."

"No problem, Mama," I say. My parents work so hard. And they never complain.

"I'll try not to ask you for too much once you're in Magnet," she says. "You'll be much busier then,

I'm sure."

"Samir will be older too. He can handle himself," Baba adds.

Not on the bus, I think. I want to tell them about Dana, but they trust me to take care of things. So I will find a way to take care of this problem too.

I stuff another bite of squash into my mouth and think, *I just have to figure out how.*

CHAPTER 7

At lunch on Monday, I watch Dana buy three cartons of strawberry milk from the lunch line and walk back to her table.

I notice something now that I didn't on the bus: Dana, Bridget, and three of the other girls at their table are all dressed alike. They wear denim vests, poofy skirts, colorful tights, and cowboy boots.

"What are they, a dance squad?" I grumble to Allie as I get back to the table.

"I like their outfits! I told Bridget that her skirt was cute."

"She looks like a cartoon."

"Come on," Allie says, rolling her eyes. I give up. Every time I say anything about Bridget, Allie defends her. "She's not that bad."

"She is. And so are her friends. How do you stand being in health class with them?"

"They're fine. I was actually Bridget's partner for a team project last week."

"Did she make you do all the work?"

"No," Allie replies. "She did her share. And she did a good job."

I don't say anything. I'm not sure what to say when Allie is always trying to tell me Bridget is actually nice. It's as if she totally forgot third grade.

Allie finally breaks the silence. "Ready for the test?" she asks me.

"What test?" I say, surprised.

"The math test—it's on the whole unit. Fractions." Allie peers at me. "You can't be worried about that. It's easy."

I'm not worried. I can multiply and divide those

things in my head. But before I can tell her that, I glance at Dana's table again. "Uh-oh," I say.

"What?" Allie asks, then looks up herself. "Oh boy."

Dana is standing by the window, walking back and forth with a fake limp, making grunting noises. I know right away that she's making fun of Ana, Samir's classmate who has cerebral palsy. Ana's family lives two streets from our house. Her father owns the coffee shop where Baba buys our bagels. Her mother helps at the animal shelter. Last Halloween, Ana and Samir dressed up as matching pumpkins. I was a farmer. We walked around our whole neighborhood for candy. The adults and I took turns pulling Ana in a little red wagon when she got too tired to walk.

Everyone at Dana's table is laughing as she stumbles around.

My hands are shaking. I put down my water bottle and stand up.

"Farah, don't go over there. Just tell someone," Allie says.

"Nobody will do anything," I answer. "They're being really awful!" I head toward Dana, marching like a soldier.

"Stay at your table!" calls the cafeteria monitor.

I ignore her. *Why hasn't she been telling Dana the same thing?* I wonder angrily.

"Where are you going, Farah?" asks Winston from his table.

I ignore him too.

"What's up, Farah?" hisses one of the Beckinson twins.

Ignore.

I even ignore Enrique, who gives me a worried look as I pass his table.

Suddenly I am standing in front of Dana and all her boot-wearing friends. Still limping, Dana doesn't notice me right away. Bridget does notice and nudges Dana.

A hush falls across the cafeteria as Dana sees me. "Pharaoh! What do *you* want?"

I hate that she calls me this name, especially now, in front of the whole cafeteria.

I see Samir outside on a bench. He's happily swinging his legs and twirling the strings of his wool hat between his fingers.

"Problem, Pharoah?"

My voice is shaking. "You're—"

"I'm what?"

"You're—"

"Yes?" She folds her arms across her chest. "Waiting, Pharaoh."

"You're a BULLY!" I shout.

Except it doesn't quite sound like a shout. More like a squeak.

The cafeteria is so quiet that we can hear the excited shrieks of the kids playing outside.

Then Dana bursts out laughing. "I'm a *bully*! Y'all hear that!" People snicker around the cafeteria. She comes up close to me and stares me right in the eyes. "Sit down, Pharaoh."

I stay.

"Now," she says in her awful whisper.

I hold my ground, feeling numb, until someone touches my elbow. It's Allie, who gently leads me back to our table. I can't believe I am doing it again—backing down. What a lousy hero I've turned out to be.

"Pathetic," says one Beckinson twin, shaking his long hair out of his eyes.

As I sit down, I see Winston run up to the cafeteria monitor. But she shrugs and tells him to go sit down. *Why do adults care more about being quiet than about being mean?* I think angrily.

"That was . . . that was . . ." I can't find the right words as I pack up my lunch lightning-quick.

"Come on, Farah Rocks," says Allie. "Focus on that unit test. Next year, we won't have to deal with her. We'll be at the Magnet Academy."

Once again, my Official Best Friend doesn't get it. "Allie," I blurt out, "but *she* will still be here. And so will Samir."

Allie looks at me like I am some creature with ten heads from Greek mythology. "But what can you do about that, Farah?" she asks. "We can tell someone. They will stop her."

I am about to say that adults here don't really seem to listen.

Then Allie adds, "But for now, we have a math test to take. And Magnet is paying attention to our grades."

Suddenly I forget to be annoyed. Because I have a great idea—an answer to my Texas-sized problem. I will give Magnet a reason not to want me. Then I'll never have to leave Samir. If they see my grades slipping, there's no way they'll accept me.

My thoughts are swirling in my head. Part of me thinks, *But you've been so excited about Magnet! How can you give that up?*

I look outside the cafeteria window. I see Samir standing on the playground, stomping his Tommy Turtle sneakers to make them light up. I'm his sister. I'm his hero.

Fifteen minutes later, I'm sitting beside Allie in class, staring at the math test Mr. Richie has handed out. The first problem states, "Multiply 4/5 by 1/3."

The answer is obviously 4/15.

I close my eyes tightly. *I'm going to do this,* I decide.

When I open my eyes, I carefully write *2/15.*

CHAPTER 8

"It's still there!" Allie says. She's peering up through the branches of the maple tree and shielding her eyes from the sun. It's the Monday after our math test, and we are at recess again, avoiding Dana.

"Where else would it be?" I mumble, stuffing my hands into my coat pockets. It's can't-feel-my-fingers-cold out here.

I'm annoyed because we are still outside when it feels like the North Pole.

I check my watch. Twelve-thirty—three minutes past our math starting time. Mr. Richie doesn't seem to mind that we're Popsicle-cold while he sips a mug of hot coffee. He's been staring at me all during recess, as if he's puzzled. I know exactly why. It's about my work on the math test. This morning Mr. Richie announced we'd be getting our tests back after recess.

Finally, he rings his brass bell. We all line up by the hopscotch court near the doors. On the other side of the playground, I see the other fifth-grade class lining up to go in. Dana is there, along with Bridget and a couple other girls. They all wear denim jackets and polka-dot blue and white skirts over navy-blue tights.

Just then, Bridget waves at Allie, who waves back slowly. "See you in health class," Bridget calls out.

"What's that about?" I ask.

"No clue."

"Are you guys friends now?"

She shrugs. "I don't know."

"They're going to freeze out here in those silly

skirts," I say. I want Allie to agree with me. I want her to say something about those popular girls so that I know she's on my side. But she doesn't say anything at all.

Inside, Mr. Richie says, "The Problem of the Day is on the board. Try to figure it out before I hand back your tests."

I'm nervous. Will Mr. Richie know that I failed last week's test on purpose? I try to imagine his face as he graded it. Did he double-check the name? Did he frown and scratch his head?

I copy the Problem of the Day into my notebook. I can solve it in my head. Numbers slide into the right places in my mind, like when Samir separates M&Ms into piles. Everything goes where it belongs. But on paper, I make up a fake answer. I even do fake work to support it.

Mr. Richie slides Allie's test onto her desk. 102/100, of course. She always does the extra credit questions. I give her a thumbs-up. She smiles and puts the test in her folder. I look up at Mr. Richie, waiting, but he's moved on to the next person. And the next and the next. Test papers, with grades in green ink, are on everyone's desks—except mine.

Mr. Richie goes to the front of the room. "Our next challenge is . . . ," he says, doing a quick drumroll on Winston's desk. "Dividing fractions!" He tells us to open our textbooks to page 124 to the sample problems.

What kind of stunt is Mr. Richie pulling? Where is my test? I think.

As if she's reading my mind, Allie whispers, "How come you didn't—"

But just then, Mr. Richie taps my shoulder. "Follow me, please, Farah Rocks."

He leads me out to the hallway. *Is he going to take me to the non-AA math class?* I wonder. *One strike and I'm out?*

Instead he leans against the lockers and peers down at me. My test is rolled up like an ancient scroll in his hand.

"Were you feeling okay on Friday, Farah?" I like how he says my name, puffing up the *h* at the end. In

September, he had a hard time with it. He kept trying until he got it right.

"I was fine," I answer. My stomach feels fluttery.

"Was something wrong?" he tries again.

"No," I lie.

"Well, I'm trying to understand this." He hands me the test paper. I unroll it and see the green ink glowing at me. *59/100.*

Holy hummus. Even though I had planned this, I am still amazed at how I feel.

Lousy.

But also weirdly proud. This fifty-nine percent is a piece of art. I created it as carefully as that bird crafted its nest in the maple tree. I showed fake work here too, so Mr. Richie could see where my calculations went "wrong."

Yet I feel awful because Mr. Richie seems so confused.

"I wish I could let you retake it," he explains. "But as you know, there are no retakes on unit tests. Try to focus on the other assignments coming up. Good grades on those should offset this one." He stares down at me. "Okay? I'd hate for this to affect your application to the Magnet Academy."

"Okay." *Close call*, I think. A retake hadn't even crossed my mind.

"Farah," he tries again, his voice quieter this time. "Is anyone bothering you here at school?"

Mr. Richie is African American, and he particularly worries about kids who aren't white and how we're doing at school. He tries to be extra aware in case someone makes us feel different, since there aren't too many of us at Harbortown. For a second, I wonder if he somehow found out about Dana.

I trust Mr. Richie, but I decide not to tell him. Ms. Juniper didn't believe me. The lunch monitor in the cafeteria did nothing. And Ms. Loft thinks Dana is a sweet girl. What would Mr. Richie do, anyway? He can't ride the bus with Samir. He can't sit in the cafeteria every day to stop Dana.

"Thanks, Mr. Richie," I say, "but nobody is bothering me."

"Okay then," he says, sounding unsure. "After school on Thursday, I'll review this material with you."

Back in the classroom, Allie whispers, "What's wrong?"

I slide into my seat and show her my score.

She gasps and runs her fingers through her hair. "What?" she demands. "You know this stuff better than I do!"

I wonder for a second if I should tell her my plan. She is my Official Best Friend, but lately she has not been acting like it. In fact, she's been becoming more and more friendly with Bridget and some of the other popular girls who are part of Dana's crew.

"Guess it was tougher than I thought," I say, shrugging.

I turn back to my classwork. From the corner of my eye, I see Allie frowning.

CHAPTER 9

I continue with my plan, although I keep it a secret. Slowly, over a week, my grades start to sink.

One day, Allie asks me during lunch if I want to study together for math. I'm pretty sure that Mr. Richie asked her to help me. He's been keeping me inside for recess to review with him.

But I don't need help with math. I need help with how to *fail* math. And Allie will never do that.

I won't ask her anyway. The other day, while working with Mr. Richie during recess, I looked out the window and saw her hanging out with Bridget by the monkey bars.

"I'm fine," I tell her now.

"Don't you care anymore about getting into Magnet?" she demands, frowning. "We're supposed to be science fair partners! And study Latin together!"

"Maybe I like it here," I say. "Even if I have to stay with people like Bridget and Dana."

"Oh, stop being angry with Bridget," she snaps. "That was a long time ago."

"I guess she really is your friend again," I snap back, angry that she's defending Bridget again.

And with that, Allie quickly packs up what's left of her lunch and storms off. I'm starting to wonder why I ever thought she understood me one hundred percent.

. . .

Later, on the bus ride home, I sneakily sit next to Samir. He's looking at a picture book about shapes. "Twapezoid," he tells me.

Bridget is sitting in the back of the bus, talking to

the Beckinson twins. "She is soooo tough," she says. Of course, she is talking about her idol, Dana.

"How tough can she be?" one of the twins scoffs. "She's a girl." (This is another reason I can't stand the Beckinsons.)

Bridget lowers her voice a bit. In my experience, when people lower their voices, they're about to say something worth hearing. I perk up and pay attention.

"Wanna know why she left her old school?" Bridget asks, as if she has supersecret information.

"Her parents got divorced, right?" Jake says, pulling his finger out of his nose.

For a flicker-quick second, I feel sad for Dana. It must have been hard to move to a new school, in a new state—and on top of that, to have your family break up.

"Not just that," Bridget says, her voice dropping even more. The Beckinsons huddle closer to her. "But there was a third grader who was trying to take Dana's spot on the basketball team, and Dana . . ." Her voice trails off.

"What?" her audience says in unison. "What did she do?"

"She grabbed her in the locker room, picked her up, and put her head in the toilet. . . ."

Suddenly I don't feel so bad for Dana.

"And what? What?" they beg.

"Yeah, what happened?" asks Winston.

I am listening so hard my ears are burning.

"She flushed it," Bridget whispers.

A round of gasps erupts, including my own.

"Duuuude . . . ," says one of the twins.

"So she got kicked out of the school," Bridget says. "And *that's* why she's at Harbortown now."

Holy hummus. Dana is worse than I ever imagined. Note to self: Avoid all school bathrooms until eighth-grade graduation.

"Fah-wah," says Samir next to me. "Look at this one. Second twapezoid."

I think about the bird's nest that is being built in the maple tree. Birds make their nests carefully, I read once.

They make them to survive rain and wind and even predators. *Samir is my little baby bird,* I remind myself. *And I am going to build a strong nest around him to keep him safe.*

I tap the book he's holding. "Trapezoid," I repeat. "Good job, habibi."

· · ·

Two nights later, Allie calls me to see if I want to do our homework together. She's trying to help me again. I tell her no.

"Why not?" she says. "We can finish fast and then hang out."

"I'm helping Mama with laundry," I lie.

Allie hesitates. "Okay," she says eventually. "Maybe next week."

I hang up, feeling weird. I wish I could tell Allie about how Dana has a talent for flushing people's heads down the toilet. This is why I cannot leave Samir alone with her. But I know she probably won't believe me now that she's getting really friendly with the popular girls.

I miss my Official Best Friend. I wish I could tell her my plan for protecting Samir. Our friendship is changing, and it's not good. I don't want that to happen, but it's happening anyway.

After I hang up with Allie, I sit down at the kitchen table to do my language arts homework. Mama is helping Samir in the bath upstairs, and Baba's washing the dishes.

For the first time ever, my homework is actually hard—only because I'm trying to invent wrong answers.

Suddenly I hear a crash and the sound of breaking glass. "A bowl?" I ask, without looking up. This is a regular event in the Hajjar household.

"Salad blate," Baba answers. He gets the broom. "Don't tell Mama, okay?"

"No broblem," I joke.

"Hey!" He laughs as he sweeps the floor. "Don't make fun of your baba, child."

Baba's hands are big and rough. I mean, he works in a quarry, cutting rocks out of the earth. His hands shouldn't wash delicate dishes, but he and Mama and I take turns because we don't have a machine dishwasher.

"She's going to make us use paper plates again," I predict. Then I turn back to my homework. Mr. Richie gave us a two-page reading assignment about the differences between seals and sea lions. There are a bunch of comprehension questions at the end.

1. **List three differences between seals and sea lions.**

I carefully write, *Seals can balance balls on their noses, their fur is shinier, and they are prettier than sea lions.*

2. **What is the main idea of this passage?**

I write, *To show how awesome seals are.*

I take a break to focus on my most important task of the night. Mama will be finished with Samir's bath soon. I only have a couple minutes.

Baba is dumping white shards of glass into the trash.

It's now or never. "Can you sign this paper for me?" I ask in a no-big-deal voice. I slide my math unit test across the table but cover the grade with my language arts homework.

"What is it?" asks Baba.

"Just a math paper," I reply, pretending to be distracted with my homework. "Parent signature, right here at the bottom." I hand him a pen.

He bends over the table, holding the dustpan in one hand and my pen in the other. "Is there a grade?" he asks.

Holy hummus, I think nervously. My heart beats fast. I get ready to snatch the paper away.

But then something saves me: I hear Mama shut off the water. She tells Samir to dry himself with the towel.

"Oh, Baba!" I say. "Samir's coming down from the bath. You should wipe the floor in case he forgets to wear his slippers. Bare feet—ouch!"

The thought of Samir running down to the kitchen and cutting his feet on an invisible sliver of glass makes

Baba panic. He scrawls his name, *Abdallah Hajjar,* on my unit test and hurries to wet a washcloth. As he kneels down to wipe the tiles, I stuff my papers into my backpack. "Thanks, Baba," I say and go to my room.

"My bleasure, habibti," he calls after me.

I sit in my room and pull out a sheet of plain paper. I carefully study Baba's signature on my math test. Then I practice writing *Abdallah Hajjar* over and over again.

As I practice, I think about how in Arabic, *habibti* means "my love." And I feel worse than ever.

Abdallah Hajjar
Abdallah Hajjar

Abdallah Hajjar
Abdallah Hajjar

Abdallah Hajjar
Abdallah Hajjar

CHAPTER 10

A few days later, I'm sitting in class doing some silent reading when Mr. Richie tells me that Ms. Loft wants to meet with me in her office.

Now my stomach starts to hurt. It's going to be hard to lie to Ms. Loft.

"Before you go," Mr. Richie says to me, "listen to the details about your team project." He explains to the class, "For our next unit, you'll be working with partners to create a lesson on fractions. Each team will make a handout and a PowerPoint. Then you'll teach it to the class."

I sigh and look at Allie. "Want to do that together?"

"Umm . . . we'll see." She stands up to walk to the pencil sharpener.

"Wait, what?" I stand up too. I'm supposed to go see Ms. Loft, but I need to find out what she means first.

We stand by the pencil sharpener. "I don't know what is happening with you," Allie whispers. "I wish you would tell me."

"Nothing," I lie.

"Farah! Please stop lying to me!" she says angrily. "First, you fail the math test. Then, you refuse to do homework with me. You don't seem to care about school at all anymore. Why should I be your partner? You might ruin my grade too!"

My mouth falls open. I don't know what to say. But a second later, I forget this conversation because I look down and notice her shoes.

Except they're not just shoes. My Official Best Friend is wearing cowboy boots.

"Why are you wearing *those*?" I blurt out.

"They're . . . they're warm," she answers.

"But you have other boots. Those are *cowboy* boots!"

Mr. Richie gives us a look. Allie scurries back to her desk before I can say anything else.

I walk down the hall to Ms. Loft's office, stunned.

Dana Denver is ruining my life. She has me terrified to get on the bus every morning. She also has me failing my classes on purpose so I can stay at Harbortown and watch out for Samir. And now my Official Best Friend is dressing like her.

Why is everything suddenly so hard?

I used to *love* school. I used to have a best friend. Now she's abandoning me for the popular crew.

As I turn the corner, I see Ms. Loft's door swing open. Someone is coming out. Someone with red hair.

"I'll try, Ms. Loft. If my grades don't go up, then I can't anymore. I'll be really upset," Dana is saying, standing in the doorway. She turns her head and sees me.

Dana glares at me. Then she turns and smiles sweetly

at Ms. Loft. "Someone's here to see you, Ms. Loft."

Ms. Loft calls out, "Thanks, honey! Tell your mom I said hello, okay?"

"I will!" Dana answers. She faces me again. "See you, Pharaoh," she says in her terrible whisper as she walks away.

Inside, Ms. Loft is filing papers. I notice a blotch of dried oatmeal on her sleeve. "Hi, Farah. Have a seat," she says.

"Hi, Ms. Loft," I answer. I sit on one of the four hard, wooden chairs near her desk.

"How are your parents? Is your mom still working?"

"Yes, she picked up more hours."

"Dad still working overtime?"

"Yes." *Come on,* I think. *Get to it.*

"It changes things sometimes, when two parents are working a lot." She looks at me as if I'm a dead bug under a microscope, smashed between two pieces of glass. "I bet you've had to help out more at home. Has it caused any . . . stress?"

Aha. There it is.

"No, not really," I say calmly. No way can I trust her now, I remind myself. She thinks Dana is a "sweet girl."

"Well, Farah, in the last two weeks, your classwork and your grades have . . . well, to be honest, they've suffered." She spreads a bunch of papers before me. I see Mr. Richie's green pen marks on several of my papers and tests, along with my faked Baba signatures.

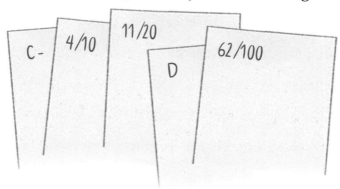

"Farah," Ms. Loft says softly, "forget about the Magnet Academy for a minute. More importantly, is anything upsetting you?"

I want to tell her. I really do. I want to say, *Yes, something is upsetting me. And it just left your office a minute ago.*

But I know nothing will change. Other adults in this building have proven that they don't think what Dana does is a big deal.

Even worse, if I complain about her, Dana might bully Samir even *more*.

Or she might actually flush my head down the toilet.

"I didn't think fifth grade would be this hard," I finally say. Lying has become really easy for me. I use my best sorry-I-disappointed-you expression.

"That surprises me." She flips through some papers on her desk. When she finds the one she's looking for, she glances up at me. "Farah, on the last standardized test, you had one of the highest scores in the whole grade. According to this," she says, tapping the paper with her index finger, "you are actually capable of doing seventh-grade work." She holds it out in front of me.

I sigh, looking sad. "Multiplying fractions is, like, really hard. And summarizing an article is not as easy as everyone thinks it is."

"I understand," she says, even though she looks really confused. "You can head back to class. I'm going to contact your parents so we can figure out how to help you get back on track."

Alarm bells go off in my head. This is something I wasn't expecting. This plan is not following a straight line like I thought it would. It's more like a labyrinth, and I have to think of a way to get out—fast.

. . .

After school my stomach is in knots as I peel an orange for Samir's snack. I'm racking my brain, trying to figure out what I'm going to tell my parents.

"Emms?" Samir asks sweetly, making me calm down right away. He's sitting at the kitchen table, using our family tablet to play an app that helps him practice his alphabet.

I smile at him. "Sorry, Samir. You have to wait until after dinner. I just peeled this orange for you, though."

I bring him the orange on a small plate. As I glance

down at the tablet, I notice a message float across the screen. Mama has a new e-mail.

"Samir, go get me your backpack, please," I say, hoping to have a minute to myself.

While Samir is out of the room, I take the tablet. I click on the mail icon and see that the e-mail is from sloft@harbortown.edu—Ms. Loft.

And then I do something I know is wrong. I open it.

Dear Mr. and Mrs. Hajjar,

I wanted to reach out to you about Farah. Her grades have been slipping drastically these past few weeks. I met with her the other day at school to check in. She says nothing is wrong, but we should discuss. Please e-mail me back or call the school. My extension is listed below. I look forward to hearing from you!

Sincerely,
Sally Loft
ext. 025

I hear Samir coming back into the kitchen. And quickly, before I really think about it, I hit *Delete*.

CHAPTER 11

On Saturday I'm reading on the couch when Mama interrupts me. "Imshee, Farah," she says. "I have to take Samir to his therapy appointment. Mrs. Liu said you could come hang out with Allie while we're gone."

I look up from my mythology book. "I didn't know that," I say.

"Mrs. Liu and I planned it," she explains. "We were talking about how you two haven't been spending time together lately."

"I don't want to go." I really don't want to see Allie, who will probably just bug me about my grades and Magnet.

Mama looks surprised. "Farah," she says sternly, "I told them you're going."

"Mama—"

"Y'Allah, bsoura'h."

I move quickly, just as she commands.

Twenty minutes later, I knock on the Lius' front door. It's a few minutes before anyone answers. Even though it's February, it's a warm day, so I don't mind waiting. But I get worried when I hear lots of shouting coming from inside. Finally, Allie yanks the door open. She yells, "Come in!" Then she disappears.

Inside the foyer, I take off my shoes. I slip my feet into a pair of guest slippers that Mrs. Liu keeps in a basket. Upstairs the entire Liu family—Mr. and Mrs. Liu, as well as Allie and her older brother, Timothy—are running around, shrieking.

"I see him!"

"Now he's in the bathroom!"

Mrs. Liu yells, "I have him!" and then more words in Chinese.

A loud screech echoes through the house.

Mr. Liu yells, "Bring me the box!"

Allie runs downstairs and picks up the cell phone on the hallway table.

"What's going on?" I ask as she dials a number.

She holds up her index finger to tell me to hold on a second. "We found him in our upstairs closet," Allie says into the phone. "Yes, please. My mom's pretty mad." She hangs up just as Mrs. Liu stomps down the steps.

Mr. Liu follows close behind. He's carrying a cardboard box. They both say hello to me quickly, but they look upset. Angry meows come from inside the box Mr. Liu is carrying. Mrs. Liu shouts in Chinese, pointing at the door with both hands.

Mr. Liu mutters something to Allie, who opens the door for him. Holding the box tightly, he stomps outside.

"Our neighbor's cat keeps getting loose," Allie explains. "This is the second time we've found her in our house. We have a broken window in the attic. That must be how she's getting in." She throws her hands in the air. "He sliced the bedroom curtains to shreds!"

At that moment, Timothy leans over the upstairs railing. "Ma! Ma! Look at my soccer jersey!"

Mrs. Liu peers up at him.

He holds up a gold and black Harbortown jersey. Actually, it's more like ribbons of fabric that *used* to be his Harbortown jersey.

"Oh no!" Mrs. Liu wails.

Just then, the neighbor arrives. "Oh, I'm just so, so sorry!" she says, poking her head inside the front door. "Little Tabby just does not want to stay put in our house."

"Let's hang out here," Allie says. She pulls me into the kitchen. "I feel bad for my mom. Last time this happened, she spent the whole day cleaning every room the cat was in. She washed every single thing it might have touched."

Mrs. Liu is a nurse and a total germaphobe. She uses boiling water to wash her floors, which are all tiled. "Carpets are hotels for bacteria!" she once told Mama, who feels the same way. Our home doesn't have carpeting either. "Only stone—beautiful, clean stone," my parents insist.

"That sounds like a lousy way to spend a Saturday," I say.

I follow Allie into the kitchen. She gets two containers of vanilla yogurt from the refrigerator and hands me a spoon.

"Seriously." Allie leans against the counter as she eats her yogurt. "What happened with your parents?"

"What do you mean?" I ask, peeling the foil that covers the yogurt container.

"Your grades!" she says. "Aren't they furious?"

"They don't really know," I say. "And I don't want them to find out." I look at her, hoping she gets my point.

"So you don't want me to tell my parents what's going on?" she asks.

"You don't need to say anything at all to them," I reply.

"That's lying."

"Not really. It's nobody's business," I say. It's silent for a minute. "Besides, I'm trying my best. My parents will understand that."

"Are you?" she asks, staring at me. "Trying your best?"

"Yeah," I say. It's getting easier and easier to lie.

We stand quietly, eating our yogurts. I can't even finish mine because my stomach starts to hurt. I feel guilty for lying, so I avoid looking at Allie. It's never been this strange hanging out with her before.

"What should we do?" she finally asks.

"Anything you want," I say. "Your house."

"We could dig for stones in the stream," she suggests. There is a pretty little creek that runs behind the Lius' house. Mr. Liu cut a path through the brush so we could reach it easily.

"Okay," I say. We put on our shoes and go outside.

As we walk, Allie says, "I drafted my Magnet essay. It was harder than I thought. Did you start yours?"

"No," I say. Then I add slowly, "Anyway, I doubt I'll get in."

"I know you're failing on purpose," Allie says flatly.

I halt in my tracks. "What did you say?"

"You know some of the math stuff better than I do," Allie says. She pushes her way past a thick bush. "And by the way, Ms. Loft called me in too—to ask what's wrong with you."

I look at my best friend in horror.

Allie stops to look back at me. "Relax," she says. "I said I didn't know anything. But I hate lying for you." She shakes her head and keeps walking toward the creek.

When we get to the creek, Allie kneels down by the water. "If this is about Dana, you shouldn't let her bother you," she says.

"She's a bully!" I protest, kneeling beside her.

Allie rakes her fingers through the water, looking for stones. "She's not that bad, you know."

What? I think. *Did my Official Best Friend really just say that Dana is "not that bad"?*

"You *must* mean she is worse than we ever imagined," I say.

"I don't think so," says Allie. She pulls out a flat, brown stone, peers at it, then tosses it back in.

"Dana Denver is a mean, awful bully, Allie Liu!" I shriek. A squirrel scuttles down a tree trunk and runs far away from us. "You're just saying this because Bridget is your friend again," I say.

"Come on," Allie says. "Bridget is not my friend. I only ever see her in school. And with Dana, it's not easy being the new kid."

"She makes fun of little kids," I remind her. "Are you okay with that?"

"Of course not," says Allie. "But it must be hard for her to be so tall. I mean, I cracked a joke about her height the first time I saw her. Plus she's on the basketball team. There's a lot of pressure."

I stay quiet and slide my fingers through the water.

Allie keeps sifting for rocks. We sit there quietly for a long time. We both look for stones, pretending to be busy so we don't have to talk. Between us, we find eight interesting ones before we decide to go back to the house. We walk along the path, not talking, each of us holding four rocks.

When we reach the back door, we see Allie's mother holding up a scrap of denim. "That bad Tabby was in your closet too!" she yells. "This belongs to your friend. The one who was here yesterday." She sighs angrily. "It's ruined."

Friend? I think. Allie hardly ever hangs out with anyone except for me.

"Don't worry, Ma," says Allie quickly. "Just put it away."

"What's her name again?" asks Mrs. Liu. "I'll have to call her mother and apologize."

"Forget it," Allie snaps. "No big deal."

I wonder why Allie is being so rude to her mom.

"I'll offer to pay for it," Mrs. Liu says. "I wonder how

much it costs." She holds up the denim, inspecting it. And suddenly I realize what the scrap of fabric is—a denim vest. I get a sinking feeling in my stomach.

"Okay, Ma. Forget it!" Allie is now practically hissing like a cat herself.

"What is her name again? Brenda?"

Allie freezes. So do I.

Mrs. Liu's face lights up. "Bridget! That's right. I'll have to call her mom and explain . . . ," she mutters as she walks up the stairs.

I drop the stones on the ground and run all the way home, ignoring Allie, who is calling me to come back.

CHAPTER 12

My favorite part of Sunday mornings is when Mama and I sit on her bed, and she brushes and braids my hair before church.

"So many tangles today," Mama murmurs. She sprays more water from a bottle onto my scalp. My hair is like hers—long, black, and totally out of control.

"I forgot to braid it when I went to sleep last night," I tell her. Every time she pulls the brush through, it pulls my head back.

"No problem. We will show it who's the boss," she says, giggling.

I laugh too. "When can we go to the labyrinth?" I ask.

"Soon. I know you've been asking to see it," Mama says. She weaves my hair into a long braid, like a thick rope, and bundles the end with a thick elastic. "Done!"

During mass, I listen to Father Alex's sermon. "Anger makes it difficult to forgive," he says. He wears a long, red cape trimmed with gold. When I was a little kid, I once asked Mama if Father Alex thought he was a superhero. (She tells *everyone* that story.)

"But we must forgive," he's saying. "Otherwise that anger can hurt us deep inside."

Here's the truth about forgiving: It's easier to *talk* about it than to actually *do* it.

I'm angry that Bridget was hanging out at Allie's house. It means that Allie has forgotten all about what Bridget did.

In kindergarten, Bridget, Allie, and I had been best friends. She played with Bubby Belly dolls, swung from the monkey bars, and collected rocks. She could kick the soccer ball around the field better than any of the boys. She used to hang out with us at Allie's house and look at stuff under Mr. Liu's microscope.

But starting in third grade, when we got back from summer vacation, she was different. Over the summer, the old Bridget had disappeared. And I didn't like the new Bridget—not one bit.

First of all, the new Bridget wore only clothes that glittered. She never wore sneakers, only flat, shiny shoes with bows on them. And lots of skirts, which meant no monkey bars anymore.

Second, she was boy-crazy. When someone asked her to play soccer, she giggled and said she didn't know how. "I'd rather watch the boys play," she said.

Third, and worst of all, she was a teaser. She told me that Bubby Belly dolls were for babies. If you wore sweatpants instead of tights, she made fun of you. "Those look like pajamas!" If you carried the same backpack from second grade to third grade, she made everyone laugh at you. "Geez, how boring!" If your mom packed you a hummus sandwich for lunch, she made a big deal. "That looks like puke!"

And if you got a good report card, like Allie and I did, she really let you have it. "What a nerd!" she would say to us both. For a while, a lot of other kids called us that too.

Here's the truth: I know I'm a nerd. And I like who I am. Maybe Allie doesn't. Maybe that's why she seems to want Bridget instead of me.

I wonder if Allie will change now too, just like Bridget did.

. . .

After dinner that night, Mama asks me again about my essay for the Magnet Academy. I pretend I don't hear her and keep polishing my rocks. I have a chunk of that red stone that Baba brought home a few days ago. I rub it harder, making it shine like a ruby.

Mama doesn't drop the subject. "Can I read what you wrote so far?"

"Not yet," I answer. I think to myself, *You probably won't have to.* I'm pretty sure the next time Ms. Loft calls me into her office, it will be to tell me that Harbortown doesn't want me to apply anymore.

"What was the topic?" Baba asks. "I don't remember it was so bery comblicated."

"It's not—not really," I say.

"You know," Mama says, turning to Baba, "Angele Baraka's son is applying. And so is Ms. Khoury's daughter, Giselle. They told me during the coffee hour today."

"Are they good students?" Baba asks.

Mama shrugs. "I'm sure they must be excellent like our Farah." She winks at me. "Straight-A girl we have."

"Yes, this girl makes me broud," Baba adds. He reaches over and ruffles my hair.

Later, in my room, Father Alex's words ring in my head. I wonder if my parents will ever forgive *me* when I don't get into the Magnet Academy.

CHAPTER 13

Friday is report card day. The teachers hand them out during last period, in small, yellow envelopes. As I climb onto the bus to go home, Ms. Juniper hands me a tiny smiley face sticker from her giant, yellow roll. I put the smiley face on my shirt. It falls off before I even get to my seat.

Samir gets a sticker that looks like a thumbs-up, which makes him happy. He hops on two feet to his seat. I take a seat across the aisle from him, staying out of Ms. Juniper's view, and watch the other kids standing in line to board the bus. My report card is sitting in my Take Home folder. I peek at it.

AA Math: C-
AA Language Arts: C+
AA Social Studies: C
AA Science: D

I've done it now. The Magnet Academy will put my application in the reject pile. Part of me feels sick, but then I look at Samir. Kindergarten kids don't get grades, just *P* for passing and *N* for needs improvement. His report card is filled with *P*'s. He's so proud of himself. And I'm proud of him.

At least Samir will have someone to watch over him, I think.

Suddenly I see a pair of purple suede boots. Two long legs in purple-striped leggings. A purple, poofy skirt and long, curly red hair.

Dana looks furious.

Wait, why is she on the bus home? I wonder. *She's supposed to be at basketball practice.*

I look down at my report card and then back up at Dana, who's holding an envelope in her hand too. And I remember her words to Ms. Loft: "If my grades don't go up, then I can't anymore." I know from Enrique that once your grades go below a C, you're off all school teams. That's why he works so hard to keep his grades high. I realize what must have happened. She must have gotten kicked off the basketball team.

Which is why she's on the bus home. It's also why she looks extra mean right now.

I try to reach across the aisle to pull Samir into my seat, but there is a wall of kids and backpacks between us.

Dana climbs aboard. "No, thanks," she mutters to Ms. Juniper, who's holding out the sticker sheet. She stomps down the aisle. And then, with a WHOMP that shakes the entire bus, Dana crashes to the floor.

The only sound for a few seconds is her water bottle. It flies out of her red backpack and rolls under one of the seats. Ms. Juniper shouts, "You okay, hon?"

Then Bridget calls, in a panicked voice, "Dana?!"

That is when I see a small foot sticking into the aisle. A small foot in a Turtle Tommy sneaker. It slips back out of the aisle, like a turtle tucking its head inside its shell. And over Dana's flattened body, Samir looks at me with his teddy-bear brown eyes.

"Uh-oh! Mean giwl down!" he blurts.

Dana stands up, her face redder than her backpack. She leans down and screeches right in Samir's face: "Are you *stupid*?"

My brother bursts into tears. Something erupts inside me. I stand up and yell, "Don't call him that!"

She turns and glares at me. "Sit down, Pharaoh."

I quiver for a second. Now Samir is crying even harder, so I find my strength again. I remain on my feet.

"Sit down, I said!" she shrieks.

"NO!" I roar. "You sit down, you bully!"

"Nerd!" she yells.

"Don't call me a nerd!" I answer, and then before

I can stop myself, I say, "Maybe if you were nerdier, you wouldn't have gotten kicked off the basketball team!"

Three things happen very quickly:

1. Dana's right hand goes up in the air. I'm pretty sure she's going to punch me right in the face.

2. Ms. Juniper yells, "NO!" from the front of the bus.

3. The other kids on the bus start chanting, "Fight! Fight!"

Now I'm even more certain that Dana is about to murder me. Without really thinking, I put both hands on Dana's shoulders and shove as hard as I can. Maybe I'm super strong. Or maybe she's not expecting it. But guess what? For the second time in two minutes, she goes crashing to the floor.

Holy. Hummus.

"Dana!" Bridget screams. Then she looks at me. "What is wrong with you, Farah?"

For once, the Beckinson twins have nothing to say.

They just stare at Dana, flat on her back, on the floor of the bus.

Samir is crying harder than ever.

And here comes Ms. Juniper, looking less like a bowling pin and more like a volcano, about to erupt.

CHAPTER 14

When my parents get home that evening, Samir and I tell them what happened on the bus. Mama's upset that Samir got his feelings hurt. Baba's furious that someone would try to bully us. Good news for me: They both forget to ask about report cards.

Later, Ms. Loft calls our house. She asks Mama and Baba to come in for a meeting with Dana and her mother.

So after lunch on Monday, I take the hall pass and head down to her office. I walk past the second-grade hallways and a window that looks onto the playground. I see the maple tree, its branches still bare. But when I peer at it, I realize something is wrong. The bird's nest is half gone. It's only shreds of vines and twigs blowing in the wind. *All that hard work is undone,* I think sadly.

In the office, Ms. Loft, Mr. Richie, and my parents all sit around a big conference table. Dana is there too. Sitting next to her is a tall, red-headed woman. She wears a navy blue suit and bright-pink lipstick.

I sit beside my mom, who is as still as a statue. Baba reaches over and holds my hand for a second. That instantly makes me feel better.

Ms. Loft explains to my parents that the bus driver saw me hit Dana so hard she fell down.

"I believe your friend was hurt," Ms. Loft says to me. Ms. Loft points to Dana, who pulls back her red curls to show a small black and blue bruise, the size of a dime, on her cheek. I press my lips together so I don't scream that Dana is an expert at flushing people's heads down the toilet.

Everyone looks at me, waiting for me to explain.

Baba smiles encouragingly at me. "Go ahead, Farah. Tell them. Tell them you didn't mean it. You were just defending yourself."

Dana's mother gasps and rolls her eyes. "Everyone *saw* you hit my daughter," she sputters angrily.

Baba puts up his hand. "Let my daughter sbeak, blease."

"You're wrong," I say to Ms. Loft. "You said I hit my friend," I say. "But Dana is *not* my friend."

Everyone stares at me, but I push on. "She's a bully," I say. "And I didn't hit her—I pushed her. If I hadn't done that, she was going to hit me and my brother."

Ms. Loft looks puzzled, so I explain. "She's been bothering Samir and me ever since her first day of school here. She calls us names and she's threatened to hurt me after school if I say anything." I explain about how she makes fun of Samir and some of his friends at lunch.

"Why didn't you tell an adult?" Ms. Loft asks.

"I told the lunch monitor. And Ms. Juniper. But

nobody took it seriously. Nobody believed it was bullying."

"She's a liar!" blurts out Dana's mother. "How dare she call my Dana a bully!"

That's when my mother finally looks up. Her eyes focus on Ms. Denver, and they are blazing. "How dare *you* accuse *my* Farah of being a liar! Do you know she's one of the hardest-working students in this school? She's in the Advanced Academic program, with straight *A*'s!"

I shrink into my seat. Mr. Richie and Ms. Loft look at each other and then at me. I know what they are thinking: *So you haven't told your parents about your grades?*

And as much as I don't like the Denver family, I think that Ms. Denver is right about one thing. I *am* a big, stinking liar.

CHAPTER 15

The school can't figure out who started the fight. And they do what adults normally do. Instead of trying to find the answer, they blame Dana *and* me. Because of that, Dana and I are *both* suspended from the bus for one week.

As we leave the office, Dana's mother takes her daughter's hand. She stomps away, her navy-blue heels clacking on the floor.

As they start to put on their coats, Mr. Richie asks my parents, "Would you mind staying for a few more minutes? There's something else we need to discuss."

My heart starts pounding really, really, really hard.

My parents are going to find out what's been happening. There is no way for me to get out of this now.

"No problem," says Mama. She and my father each kiss me. "I'll pick you up after school since you can't ride the bus. Okay?"

"Uh, okay," I say nervously.

Baba wraps his arm around me. "Sometimes kids act so tough because they have a lot of hurt inside them," he says. "I think maybe this girl has some hurt. But even so, I'm broud of you for brotecting your brother," he tells me. He and Mama follow Ms. Loft and Mr. Richie back into the office.

For the whole day, I worry. I imagine my parents' faces when they hear about my grades. I know for a fact they will be furious when they realize I've been lying to them. And faking signatures. And deleting e-mails.

Holy hummus, I think. *How did I get myself into this mess?*

When I leave school, Mama is sitting in the car

pickup line. I open the car door and climb in. "Hi," I say nervously. I watch her face for clues.

"Hello, Farah," she says. Not *habibti*. Not *sweetheart*. Just Farah.

After a moment, she says something that surprises me. "Let's go do something special. The bus won't drop off Samir until three-twenty. We have thirty-five minutes by ourselves. Just the Hajjar girls."

"Okay," I say hesitantly.

We drive to the public library, and I realize we're going to see the labyrinth.

I'm so excited I can barely speak. It's just what I pictured—a huge, circular maze the size of a baseball field. We hold hands and start at the entrance, winding our way through.

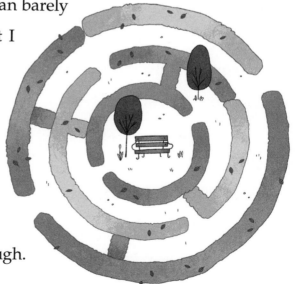

It takes us ten minutes to get to the center, where there is a bench.

"I love it," I tell Mama. "Let's come here every day." I sit down on the bench.

"Inshallah," she says, sitting beside me.

"I'm going to tell Baba we should build one like it in our backyard," I add.

"Sounds fun," she agrees. "Our whole family has been like this lately, right? Going through a big maze." Because her voice gets serious, I know that now it's time for us to have an Important Talk.

"Farah, I'm feeling angry. And really confused," she begins. "First of all, you know you can never, ever again fake my or Baba's signature, right?"

"Yes."

She pauses. "Second, your grades. You did not suddenly become a D student. I think maybe we pressured you too much about Magnet." Before I can say anything, she continues. "Farah, your baba never finished high school, because he had to work with your grandfather.

They were so poor. And when he came to America, he was always working, working."

"But *you* went to college, right?" I ask her.

"Oh, Farah." She sighs. "I went to college for one year. Just one. And then your grandfather, my father, lost his job in the factory. I have four sisters and two brothers. He couldn't spend all that money on me. So I left school to work. We saw the Magnet Academy as a big chance for you." She stands up and reaches for my hand. "But if you don't want to attend," she says with a shrug, "we cannot force you. We don't want to push you if you'll be unhappy there."

Suddenly I feel ridiculous for ruining my grades. It's as if I have thrown away all my parents' hard work. "Is that what you think? That I don't want to go?" I ask.

"Farah, you are doing badly in school on purpose. What other reason could there be?"

"It was all because of Dana! I was only trying to protect Samir." I place my elbows on my knees and cover my face with my hands. "She was awful, awful, awful.

And the adults didn't seem to care." I tell her everything that's happened, in detail: the poking, the laughing in the cafeteria, Pharaoh, the toilet-flushing story.

"Sounds like you were really scared," she says, putting her arm around me. "I thought this girl was just a problem one time on the bus. Why didn't you tell me?"

"Baba was upset about not getting a raise. And you're working more hours. I was trying to take care of it myself," I say, my voice cracking. I feel hot tears under my eyelids, trying to come out. I blink them away. "You always say I should watch out for Samir."

She holds me tightly, then gently pulls my hands away from my face so she can kiss my cheek. "That doesn't mean you are alone. We solve problems *together*, habibti," she says.

We're quiet while I think about her words. "Dana acts like an angel around grown-ups," I mumble.

Mama shakes her head. "Yes, I know kids like that."

I exhale in relief. I knew my mother would understand.

"If I go to Magnet, she will find a way to bully him. I know it!" I say.

"But Farah," she says, hugging me close, "protecting Samir is *my* job. And Baba's job. If you go to Magnet, *we* will make sure Samir is okay at Harbortown."

I'm quiet as we weave our way back through the maze and then as we drive home. I think through everything that's happened. My fight with Allie, Samir being bullied, *me* being bullied, my failing grades.

Mama understood me so well just now at the labyrinth. I should have known that she wouldn't be like Ms. Juniper or the lunch monitor. I should have known that, even though she and Baba seem tired and stressed, they would have made sure Samir was safe. I don't have to solve everything on my own.

We pull in to our driveway just as the bus arrives. Samir clambers down. Ms. Juniper gives me an odd wave, and I wave back at her. I see Bridget's face in the window. She's sitting alone, and she's glaring at me.

That night at dinner, Baba gives me his own version

of an Important Talk. It's shorter than Mama's. "You are a good sister to Samir. *But,*" and he pauses, "even if you think you cannot talk to anyone at school, you can still talk to me and your mama. The Hajjars don't keep secrets from each other."

"Yes," I say, looking down at my plate.

"*And . . . ,*" he says, "don't you eber, eber again forge my signature. There is only one Abdallah Hajjar in this house. *Me.*"

That night, before bedtime, I lie on my bed and make a list.

O   O   O   O   O   O   O

HOW CAN I FIX THIS PROBLEM?

1. Make sure to apologize to Mr. Richie and Ms. Loft.

2. Apologize to Mama and Baba every day for at least a hundred years.

3. Figure out whether or not I still have an Official Best Friend.

4. Try really, really hard to get into Magnet.

Going to Magnet is what I've always wanted, and I still want it. I really want to go to a science fair every month. And I want to learn Latin!

But there are two problems. My awful, rotten, stinking grades and the essay I still haven't written.

I dig the essay form out of a pile and read the question again: *In three hundred words or less, explain what you can contribute to Magnet Academy's student body.*

I get an idea, and I pull out a new sheet of paper. *Maybe,* I think, *I can put the two problems together and solve them at the same time.*

I begin writing.

CHAPTER 16

The next day, I go to Ms. Loft's office during my lunch period. She is standing by the file cabinet. A Cheerio is glued to her elbow with dried milk.

"Hello, Farah." She actually seems happy to see me. "Sit down." She pulls a chair close to her desk. "I've been waiting to solve this mystery."

My throat feels as dry as dust, but I try to explain. "Even you seemed to think Dana was awesome. I didn't think you'd believe me if I told you what she was doing."

"I would have listened, Farah," she says.

"But Dana is your neighbor! You said she was a really nice girl."

"Farah, you didn't even give me a chance to help."
She says this softly, and I know she is right. I think
about what Mama said about how protecting Samir is
her and Baba's job too, and that I should have told them.
I didn't even give them a way to help me. I just tried to
fix it all on my own.

"I really do want to go to Magnet," I tell her. "Did I
ruin everything?"

"Well, the essay is a big factor, and you're a great
writer." She takes the draft that I hand to her. "I'll read
this and give you some suggestions. But
Farah," she adds, "don't get your hopes up."

Now I feel like a deflated balloon.
"There's something else I need from you
too," I tell her.

She glances up. "What's that?"

"We have a bully problem," I say,
"and adults don't always listen."

"I'm listening now," she says.

And together, we make a plan.

. . .

I walk down the hallway to the Reading Room. I'm starving, and now I only have about ten minutes to eat my lunch.

The light is already on. Someone is sitting in my favorite spot by the crystal. It's Allie, and she has her shiny, black hair in a ponytail. I suddenly feel nervous and shy.

"Hi, Farah Rocks," she says. She points at the crystal. "What kind is this?"

I sit down. "Just plain quartz."

"Oh," she says, picking up a chunk of sushi with her chopsticks. "Not feldspar?"

"Nope." I unzip my lunch pouch.

"So what happened on the bus?" she asks.

"Didn't your best friend, Bridget, tell you about it?" I know I'm being rude, but I can't help it.

"Come on, Farah." Allie puts down her chopsticks. "She's not my best friend, and you know it." She sighs. "I heard you got suspended from the bus. I was so worried."

I stay quiet and just eat the sandwich that Mama packed for me.

"You know," Allie says after a few minutes, "a few days ago, I figured out Bridget's plan. She was only pretending to be my friend so I could tutor Dana. She was afraid she'd get kicked off the basketball team, so Bridget thought she'd use me to help."

I don't answer.

"I wanted to tell you. I thought you could help me figure out what Bridget was up to. But it's been hard to talk to you lately. You've been acting so weird."

I don't say anything. My throat closes up on me, like I could cry at any second. I've done to Allie exactly what I did to my parents and my teachers. I totally blocked her out and didn't let her help me. She wanted to be a friend, but I didn't let her.

So many thoughts swirl around in my head that my mouth doesn't seem to work. Eventually, because I'm not talking, Allie packs up her lunch pouch and leaves.

I want to call her back and say, "I'm sorry!" but my tongue feels like a heavy rock in my mouth.

. . .

During language arts, Mr. Richie hands me a copy of the grammar quiz. We have to make sure the nouns and the pronouns agree. There are forty questions.

"Just do your best," he says kindly to me.

I bring it back seven minutes later, while everyone else is still working. He scans my answers, then looks up at me. His eyes sparkle like polished stones. "Welcome back, Farah Rocks," he says, grinning.

Since I finish early, I take the hall pass and go to the bathroom. While washing my hands, I study my face in the mirror.

It's been a strange week, but now that the old Farah is back, I feel better. Except for Allie, things feel normal again.

Suddenly another face appears behind me in the mirror. A face that is framed with red hair.

Holy hummus, I think. *She's going to flush my head, right here, right now, and there will be no witnesses.*

Swiveling around, I try not to panic. She glares at me, and I put my hands up in front of me. If Dana is going to flush me, she's going to get the fight of her life.

"Chill out, Pharaoh," she says. She approaches the sink, keeping her distance from me. "I'm not going to touch you."

"What do you want?" I snap.

"To use the bathroom. Duh." She doesn't go into a stall, though. She just stands in front of the mirror and pulls a lip gloss tube from her pocket. "Enjoying your bus suspension?"

"It's okay." I inch toward the door. She doesn't come after me. "I'm going back to class."

"Well, *I'm* going back to Texas." She slides the pink lip gloss across her lips. "My parents might get back together." Then she does something weird—she *smiles.* "The suspension freaked them both out. They think their separation is hurting me." She laughs. "So my dad wants us to come back. We're leaving in a few weeks." She enters the stall. I hear the lock bar slide into place.

"Okay, well, see you," I say awkwardly.

"See you, Pharaoh!" she calls out.

As I walk back to class, I think about how I might now understand why Dana is a bully.

But I'm still glad she's moving back to Texas.

. . .

After school, I stop by Ms. Loft's office. She returns my Magnet Academy essay with some comments. "Thank you so much," I say.

She adds, "And I'm working on my end of the deal."

That evening, I type the essay up on our family computer. I use Ms. Loft's fixes and check my spelling along the way. Here's what I write:

Dear Admissions Officer:

I may not seem like the perfect candidate for the Magnet Academy, especially if you look at my third quarter report card. But the Magnet Academy would be a super opportunity for me.

And for you.

Until the second quarter, my grades were always straight A's. Not because I'm a nerd, which is what some people at my school will tell you. And not because I eat a lot of hummus, which the ladies at church say is good for my brain.

It's because I love to learn. You should see my rock collection in my room. I like math too. Numbers dance around in my head all the time. They make patterns that I can see. I can read a chapter book in one day (if it's a Saturday).

Do you know what else I love as much as I love to learn? My family. I especially love my little brother, Samir, even though some people don't really understand him. He was born too early, and that's why he has some challenges. But some people see only his challenges. They don't understand how smart and funny he actually is.

I was worried about leaving Samir alone at Harbortown Elementary/Middle School. We had a bully problem, and he was teased a lot. I thought I could protect my brother if I stayed at Harbortown with him. I started to do badly in classes on purpose, so that I wouldn't be accepted to your amazing school.

I'm learning that I have to let other people know when I need help, instead of always trying to do everything myself.

I hope you'll ignore, if you can, my third quarter grades. (Try hard!) Think about this essay, or my first and second quarter report cards, or my entrance test.

I promise, if you let me attend the Magnet Academy, I'll be a hardworking student who treats everyone with kindness. Because being kind is as important as being smart.

Yours sincerely,

Farah Hajjar
(Farah Rocks)

I hit *Print* and slip the paper into a large, yellow envelope. I'm sad, because I doubt I will be accepted. But I'm also relieved. At least I can say I tried my best. That's what the old Farah would have done.

The old Farah would have also shown this essay to Allie before mailing it. But I'm afraid I've ruined that friendship forever.

And that makes me sadder than anything else.

CHAPTER 17

On Thursday, I stay after school. I hang out in the library and finish my homework. Then, at exactly four p.m., I head to the cafeteria. The teachers and staff have their weekly meeting today, and I am going to be their special guest.

Mr. Richie is there. Ms. Juniper and the bus drivers, who've just finished dropping off all the kids, are there too. So is the lunch monitor, even though she's not wearing her blue apron.

Ms. Loft leads the meeting. "We have had a bully problem at Harbortown for the last several weeks," she explains. "And even though we talk about bullying a lot, we missed it this time." She turns to me. "Fifth grader Farah Hajjar wants to say something to us, from a student's point of view."

I stand up, and then I freeze. There sure are a *lot* of people in this room. Mr. Richie waves at me and gives me a thumbs-up. I suck in a deep breath, exhale, and start talking.

"As students, we always hear that we should tell you if there's a bullying problem. But sometimes we think of bullying in *big* ways. Like, maybe you imagine someone getting stuffed in a locker. Or someone getting pounded in the face on the playground. But bullying happens in other ways too. Quieter ways."

I explain what happened on the bus for the past month. While I describe the poking and the name-calling, I notice Ms. Juniper in the back. She looks sad.

Ms. Loft tells everyone we should discuss what I've said. Mr. Richie speaks first. He thinks Harbortown needs to handle bully reports differently. "We should interview the kids separately first," he says, "*before* we put them together. This way, everyone feels comfortable telling us the whole story."

Ms. Loft says she will look into the school code to see if there's more advice on how to do this. And Ms. Juniper raises her hand to say that she will ask her supervisor how drivers should handle problems on the bus.

After the meeting, Mr. Richie stands with me outside on the curb, waiting for Mama to pick me up. "I'm glad you spoke in our meeting today," he tells me. "Sometimes adults forget what it was like to be a kid."

"I should've told you what was happening."

"You're a smart girl," he says, shrugging. "You probably thought you could handle it on your own."

"Yeah. I did think that. But I was wrong."

At that moment, we see Mama's car pulling up.

"I sent in my Magnet application," I say. "Keep your fingers crossed for me!"

"For sure, Farah Rocks!" Mr. Richie says. He smiles as I get into the car, then waves as we drive away.

. . .

The next day at recess, Allie is kneeling under the maple tree. I haven't really seen her since we met in the Reading Room last week. I've told Mama about how I lied to Allie too. She said that I owed my Official Best Friend an apology.

"It might not fix everything, but it's still the right thing to do," she told me last night.

"Hey. What are you doing?" I ask Allie now.

She looks up. In her hands are twigs and small stems from leaves. "Collecting scraps."

"For what?"

"For the bird." She points up at the tree. I look up and see that the bird has started a new nest. "I think she'll see it if I put it in the corner of that branch," she says.

Standing on her tiptoes, she crams the clump of twigs into the elbow of the branch. "There." She claps her hands together to knock off the dirt.

"I'm sorry for lying to you," I blurt out. "And for

running off that day at your house. I wish I had told you what was happening."

"Why didn't you?" she asks.

"I guess I thought you were becoming friends with Bridget again. And you kept saying Dana wasn't so bad. I thought you didn't really get it. You didn't see how much they bothered me."

"I'm sorry too. I should've been a better friend," Allie says. "But after a while, I thought *you* didn't want to be *my* friend anymore."

Holy hummus, I think. I didn't realize I'd made Allie feel that way.

"Sorry—a hundred times," I say.

"Sorry—a million times," she says back.

We sit together under the tree, and I tell her all the details I have kept secret from her. She especially wants to know about the fight and how I spoke at the teachers' meeting about bullying.

"You know," Allie says when I finish, "I still can't believe you did what you did." She shakes her head.

"You failed tests and quizzes to get bad grades. *On purpose!*"

"It was actually hard work," I tell her. "I'm kind of gifted at that."

She looks stunned and then bursts out laughing.

And that's it—we're Official Best Friends again.

That's the thing about real best friends. Once you forgive, everything goes right back to normal.

MAGNET
ACADEMY

Farah Hajjar
5 Hollow Woods Lane
Granite, PA 19100

Dear Ms. Hajjar,

The Magnet Academy is pleased to accept your application to its sixth-grade class! Congratulations! This is a major recognition of your academic achievement.

We were very impressed with your personal essay. It shows good character. You will make a great addition to our school.

There is a student and parent orientation in August, at which you will learn more about our school.

Get ready for a great year!

Sincerely,
The Magnet Academy

Farah's Holy Hummus Recipe

Ingredients:

- 8-oz. can chickpeas
- 2 Tbsp tahini (sesame seed paste)
- 2 Tbsp lemon juice
- pinch of salt
- 1/2 tsp ground cumin

- 4 Tbsp water
- 1 Tbsp olive oil
- pinch of paprika
- pita bread, wheat crackers, or vegetables

Equipment:

- can opener
- blender or food processor
- spoon
- plate

What to Do:

1. Ask an adult to help you open the can of chickpeas and drain the water. Rinse out the beans in a bowl and put them in a food processor.

2. Add the tahini, lemon juice, salt, cumin, and water. Blend the ingredients together until you have a creamy texture.

3. Use a clean spoon to taste your hummus. Add anything else that seems to be missing. Maybe more salt? More lemon? It's *your* hummus, so make it the way you like it!

4. Remove your hummus and spread it onto a flat plate. Drizzle the olive oil over it and sprinkle with paprika to decorate.

5. Eat with pita bread, crackers, or veggies! Sometimes Samir and I put it in a sandwich (like peanut butter) and enjoy it that way!

Glossary

academic (ak-uh-DEM-ik)—having to do with learning

achievement (uh-CHEEV-ment)—a thing done successfully

annoyance (uh-NOI-yuhns)—the feeling of being irritated

apologize (uh-PAH-luh-jize)—to say that you're sorry for something

cemetery (SEM-i-tair-ee)—a place where dead people are buried

cerebral palsy (seh-REE-bruhl PALL-see)—a condition that is caused by damage to the brain around the time of birth

chopsticks (CHAHP-stiks)—a pair of thin sticks used for handling food

confident (KAHN-fi-duhnt)—having a strong belief in your own abilities

Gospel (GAHS-puhl)—one of the four books in the New Testament of the Bible, which tell the story of Jesus's life and his teachings

mythology (mi-THAH-luh-jee)—a group of stories that belong to a particular culture or religion

occupational therapist (ahk-yuh-PAY-shuhn-uhl THER-uh-pist)—a trained professional who helps people learn to do the activities of daily life

offset (awf-SET)—to make up for

pharaoh (FAIR-oh)—the title given to kings in ancient Egypt

quarry (KWOR-ee)—a place where stone or sand is dug from the ground

stonecutter (STONE-kuht-er)—a person who cuts stone from a quarry

sushi (SOO-shee)—a Japanese dish made of small cakes of rice with raw fish or vegetables, wrapped in seaweed

tattle (TAT-uhl)—to tell someone in charge that someone else is doing something wrong

❀ Glossary of Arabic Words ❀

ahmar—red

al-madrasa—school

aziza—dear

biddee—I want

bintkoum—your daughter

bsoura'h—quickly

farah—joy

habibi—my love (to a boy)

habibti—my love (to a girl)

hajjar—rocks

hilou—pretty

imshee—walk

inshallah—God willing, or I hope so

koosa mahshi—stuffed squash

mean—who

samir—a person who's fun to be around

y'Allah—slang for "hurry up" or "let's go"